Pamela Duncan Edwards

Dinosaur
Starts School

illustrated by
Deborah Allwright

MACMILLAN CHILDREN'S BOOKS

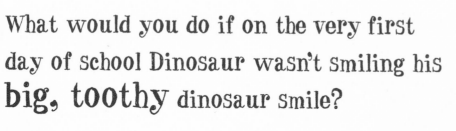

What would you do if on the very first
day of school Dinosaur wasn't smiling his
big, toothy dinosaur smile?

School

First published 2008 by Macmillan Children's Books
a division of Macmillan Publishers Limited
20 New Wharf Road, London N1 9RR
Basingstoke and Oxford
Associated companies throughout the world
www.panmacmillan.com

ISBN: 978-1-4050-3510-1 (hb)
ISBN: 978-1-4050-3511-8 (pb)

A CIP catalogue record for this book is available from the British Library.

Printed in Belgium by Proost

For Margaret and David Minch
and all those wonderful
grandchildren,
with love P. D.E.

For Pablo and Oscar,
with love D.A.

You'd say, "Don't worry, Dinosaur.
School will be **fun!**"

What if he **stamped** his feet

and **roared** in his
loudest dinosaur voice,

RROOARR!

"But dinosaurs don't
have to go to school!"

You'd say, "Of course they do, Dinosaur. Otherwise how would dinosaurs grow up to be so clever?"

What if you got to the school gates but Dinosaur wrapped his sharp claws around the railings and said in his timid dinosaur voice, "But it's too **big**. I'll get lost."

You'd say, "Silly old thing!
You can't get lost because our classroom
is just the right size for dinosaurs."

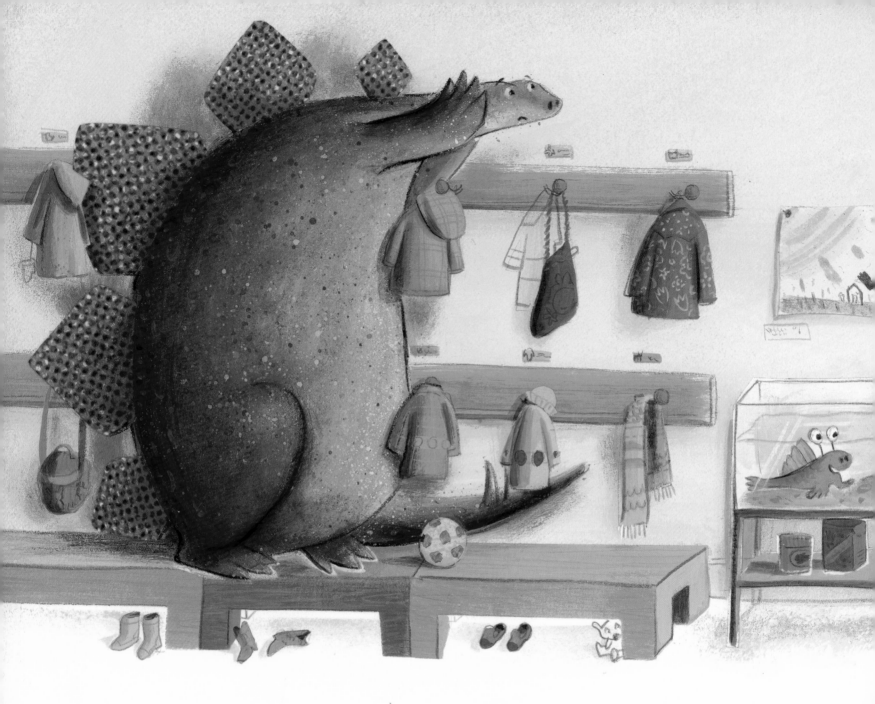

What if you reached the classroom door but Dinosaur
covered his tiny ears and said in his quiet dinosaur voice,
"But it's too **noisy.** I'll get a headache."

You'd say, "It's only noisy because everyone is laughing and having a good time."

What if the teacher asked everyone to say their names?

What if Dinosaur turned away and tried to hide under the table?

You'd say, "I think you should tell the teacher your name, Dinosaur. She might think you're not here and give someone else your crayons by mistake."

What if you were painting
pictures of the sun but Dinosaur
got in a bit of a mess?

What if his bright dinosaur eyes filled
with tears and he began to cry?

You'd say, "Wow, Dinosaur! You've made sunbeams
come out of your sun. I wish I'd thought of that."

What if it was time for lunch but Dinosaur said in his worried dinosaur voice, "They might give us something yucky to eat."

You'd say, "We'll tell them that some dinosaurs are herbivores and don't like meat. Then you can leave your sausages and just have salad instead."

What if everyone ran out to play but Dinosaur hid behind you and looked shy?

What if you and Dinosaur noticed someone else looking shy, too?

I bet Dinosaur would whisper in his gentlest dinosaur voice,
"Shall we play on the swings together?"

Then you and Dinosaur and your new friend would
have a great time pushing each other on the swings.

You'd take turns on the seesaw.

You'd build a castle in the sandpit.

You'd play chase until you
were giggling so hard you
couldn't run any more.

What if at the end of the day you said, "I told you school was fun, Dinosaur. Shall we come back again tomorrow?"

I bet he'd nod his handsome dinosaur head.

Then I bet he'd smile his
big, toothy dinosaur smile.

And I bet that you'd
smile right back.

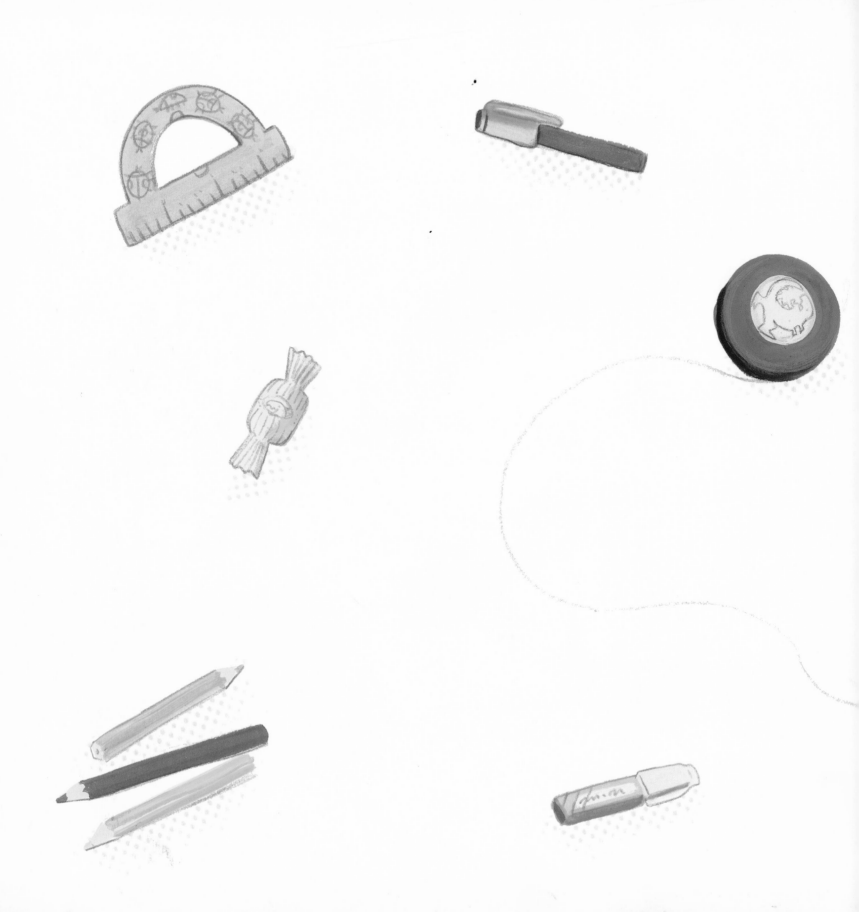